Pre-school Child

Pre-school Child

By

Dinesh Veerma

Worldwide Published by
□ **Pendown** Press

PENDOWN PRESS

An ISO 9001 & ISO 14001 Certified Co.,

Regd. Office: 2525/193, 1st Floor, Onkar Nagar-A,
Tri Nagar, Delhi-110035

Ph.: 09350849407, 09312235086

E-mail: info@pendownpress.com

Branch Office: 1A/2A, 20, Hari Sadan, Ansari Road,
Daryaganj, New Delhi-110002

Ph.: 011-45794768

Website: PendownPress.com

First Edition: 2013

ISBN: 978-93-81970-60-7

Layout and Cover Designed by Pendown Graphics Team

Printed and Bound in India by Thomson Press India Ltd.

Dedicated
to all the parents for enhancing their child...

Foreword

The first five years of a child's life are a time of tremendous physical, emotional, social and cognitive growth. Children enter the world with many needs in order to grow: love, nutrition, health, social and emotional security and stimulation in the important skills that prepare them for school success. Children also enter the world with a great capacity to learn.

Research shows clearly that children are more likely to succeed in learning when their families actively support them. Families who involve their children in activities that allow the children to talk, explore, experiment and wonder show that learning is both enjoyable and important. They motivate their children to take pleasure in learning and to want to learn more. They prepare them to be successful in school — and in life. There is a strong connection between the development a child undergoes early in life and the level of success that the child will experience later in life. When young children are provided an environment rich in language and literacy interactions and full of opportunities to listen to and use language constantly, they can begin to acquire the essential building blocks for learning how to read. A child who enters school without these skills runs a significant risk of starting behind and staying behind.

This book includes activities for families with children from infancy through age 5. Most of the activities make learning experiences out of the everyday routines in which you and your child already participate. Mostly use materials that are found in your home or that can be had free of charge from your local library. The activities are designed to be fun for both you and your child as well as to help your child gain the skills needed to get ready for school.

Few Words

Pre-schoolers are constantly on the move, exploring their world with exuberance, curiosity, and a seemingly endless source of energy. A child's capacity for learning in this stage is enormous. Pre-school-age children learn and develop from every experience, relationship, and adventure they encounter. Having the space and opportunity to explore objects and play environments helps pre-school children develop their imagination and master the motor, cognitive, language, and social skills that are essential for future development.

The pre-school years are an exciting time for young children. When they were infants, they developed a trust of their caregivers. As toddlers, they began to establish some independence. Now, as preschoolers, they use this trust and independence to actively explore new forms of play and new environments.

Adults play an important role in helping children take initiative and explore their environments. Adults' behaviors, attitudes and styles of thinking contribute to preschoolers' development. Talking with children and including them in conversations helps to develop their language skills. It is important to give children opportunities for make-believe play. This helps them to understand themselves and others, and encourages their imaginations.

This work will provide a helping hand to parents who are in need to understand their pre-schoolers.

–Dinesh Veerma

Acknowledgement

I am but a medium the true writer of this work is the Almighty, without whose blessings and guidance, the book could have never taken shape. After all, man proposes and HE disposes...

I would like to put in my appreciation and acknowledgement for some people without whom the project wouldn't have seen light. My parents, Mr. Mahesh Chand and Mrs. Bimla Devi, for their constant support and trust in me, my wife, Mrs. Anita Verma and my daughter Tanya and Bhuvi, for standing by me through thick and thin.

I would also like to acknowledge Mrs. Jinnie Gogia Chugh, editor, for giving valuable inputs.

No work can find success without the most important part, that is, YOU, The READERS. I wholeheartedly thank the readers for having spent their precious time in giving this work a fair reading. Life is a struggle, and we need to consistently work, and grab the opportunities that come in our way and set parameters for our achievements and goals. The work is especially dedicated to those, who see success not as a destination, but as a journey and a way of life.

- Author

Contents

CHAPTER 1

Introduction

Children are storehouses of talent. The little infants, when come to the world are pure and godly creatures, full of untapped energy and enthusiasm.

Scientists who study how the brain works have shown that children learn earlier—and learn more—than we once thought possible. From birth through age 5, children are developing the language, thinking, cognitive, physical, emotional and social skills that they will need for the rest of their lives.

This book is for families and caregivers who want to help their pre-school children to learn and to develop the skills necessary for success in school—and in life.

The book begins with information that will help you prepare your child to learn and to get ready for school. The major portion of the book contains simple activities that you can use with your child. These activities are only a starting point. We hope that you and your child will enjoy them enough to create and try many more on your own.

In addition, the book provides suggestions for how to monitor your child's TV viewing and to choose good TV programs and videos and how to choose suitable child care. It also provides a checklist to guide you as you prepare your child to enter kindergarten.

As a parent, you can help your child want to learn in a way no one else can. That desire to learn is a key to your child's later success. Enjoyment is important! So, if you and your child don't enjoy one activity, move on to another. You can always return to any activity later on.

CHAPTER 2

Ready to Learn

How well children will learn and develop and how well they will do in school depends on a number of things, including the children's health and physical well-being, their social and emotional preparation and their language skills and general knowledge of the world.

Good Health and Physical Well-Being

Seeing to it that your pre-school child has nutritious food, enough exercise and regular medical care gives him a good start in life and lessens the chances of him having health problems or trouble learning later on.

Food

Pre-schoolers require a healthy diet. After your child is born, he requires nutritious food to keep him healthy. School-aged children can concentrate better in class if they eat balanced meals that include servings of breads and cereals; fruits and vegetables; meat, poultry and fish and meat alternatives (such as eggs and dried beans and peas); and milk, cheese and yogurt. You should see to it that your child does not eat too many fatty foods and sweets.

Children aged 2-5 generally can eat the same foods as adults but in smaller portions. Your child's doctor or medical clinic adviser can provide you with advice on what to feed a baby or a toddler who under the age of 2.

If you need food for your child, national, state and local programs can help. For example, the several nutrition programs distribute food to low-income women and their children across the country.

Exercise

Pre-schoolers need opportunities to exercise. To learn to control and coordinate the large muscles in his arms and legs, your child needs to throw and catch balls, run, jump, climb and dance to music. To learn to control and coordinate the small muscles in his hands and fingers, he needs to color with crayons, put together puzzles, use blunt-tipped—safety—scissors, zip his jacket and grasp small objects such as coins.

If you suspect that your child has a disability, see a doctor as soon as possible. Early intervention can help your child to develop to his full potential.

Medical Care

Pre-schoolers require regular medical checkups, immunizations and dental care. It's important for you to find a doctor or a clinic where your child can receive routine health care as well as special treatment if he becomes sick or injured.

Early immunizations can help to prevent a number of diseases including measles, mumps, German measles (rubella), diphtheria, tetanus, whooping cough, hib (Haemophilus influenzae type b), polio and tuberculosis. These diseases can have serious effects on your child's physical and mental development. Talk to your doctor about the benefits and risks of immunization.

Beginning by the age of 3 at the latest, your child also should have regular dental checkups. Oral hygiene and health is very important.

Social and Emotional Preparation

Children start school with different degrees of social and emotional maturity. These qualities take time and practice to learn. Give your child opportunities at home to begin to develop the following positive qualities:

- **Confidence:** Children must feel good about themselves and believe that they can succeed. Confident children are more willing to attempt new tasks—and try again if they don't succeed the first time.

- **Independence:** Children must learn to do things for themselves.

- **Motivation:** Children must want to learn.

- **Curiosity:** Children are naturally curious and must remain so to get the most out of learning opportunities.

- **Persistence:** Children must learn to finish what they start.

- **Cooperation:** Children must be able to get along with others and learn to share and take turns.

- **Self-control:** Children must learn that there are good and bad ways to express anger. They must understand that some behaviors, such as hitting and biting, are not acceptable.

- **Empathy:** Children must have an interest in others and understand how others feel.

- **Belief:** They must believe in themselves and be sure of your trust in them at every step.

Here are some things that you can do to help your child develop these qualities:

- Show your child that you care about him and that you are dependable. Children who feel loved are more likely to be confident. Your child must believe that, no matter what, someone will look out for him. Give your baby or toddler plenty of attention, encouragement, hugs and lap time.

- Set a good example. Children imitate what they see others do and what they hear others say. When you exercise and eat nourishing food, your child is more likely to do so as well. When you treat others with respect, your child probably will, too. If you share things with others, your child also will learn to be thoughtful of others' feelings.

- Provide opportunities for repetition. It takes practice for a child to crawl, pronounce new words or drink from a cup. Your child doesn't get bored when he repeats things. Instead, by repeating things until he learns them, your child builds the confidence he needs to try new things.

- Use appropriate discipline. All children need to have limits set for them. Children whose parents give them firm but loving discipline generally develop better social skills and do better in school than do children whose parents set too few or too many limits. Here are some ideas:

  - Direct your child's activities, but don't be too bossy.

  - Give reasons when you ask your child to do something. Say, for example, "Please move your car from the stairs so no one falls over it"—not, "Move it because I said so."

  - Listen to your child to find out how he feels and whether he needs special support.

- Show love and respect when you are angry with your child. Criticize your child's behavior but not the child. Say, for example, "I love you, but it's not okay for you to draw pictures on the walls. I get angry when you do that."

- Help your child make choices and work out problems. You might ask your 4-year-old, for example, "What can we do to keep your brother/sister from knocking over your blocks?"

- Be positive and encouraging. Praise your child for a job well done. Smiles and encouragement go much further to shape good behavior than harsh punishment.

• Let your child do many things by himself. Young children need to be watched closely. However, they learn to be independent and to develop confidence by doing tasks such as dressing themselves and putting their toys away. It's important to let your child make choices, rather than deciding everything for him.

• Encourage your child to play with other children and to be with adults who are not family members. Pre-schoolers need social opportunities to learn to see the point of view of others. Young children are more likely to get along with teachers and classmates if they have had experiences with different adults and children.

- Show a positive attitude towards learning and towards school. Children come into this world with a powerful need to discover and to explore. If your child is to keep his curiosity, you need to encourage it. Showing enthusiasm for what your child does ("You've drawn a great picture!") helps to make him proud of his achievements.

Children also become excited about starting school when their parents show excitement about this big step. As your child gets ready to enter kindergarten, talk to him about school. Talk about the exciting things that he will do in kindergarten, such as making art projects, singing and playing games. Be enthusiastic as you describe all the important things that he will learn from his teacher—how to read, how to count and how to measure and weigh things.

Language and General Knowledge
Children can develop language skills only if they have many opportunities to talk, listen and use language to solve problems and learn about the world.

Long before your child enters school, you can do many things to help him develop language. You can:

- **Give your child opportunities to play.** Play is how children learn. It is the natural way for them to explore, to become creative, to learn to make up and tell stories and to develop social skills. Play also helps children learn to solve problems—for example, if his wagon tips over, a child must figure out how to get it upright again. When they stack up blocks, children learn about colors, numbers, geometry, shapes and balance. Playing with others helps children learn how to negotiate.

- **Support and guide your child as he learns a new activity.** Parents can help children learn how to do new things by "scaffolding," or guiding their efforts. For example, as you and your toddler put together a puzzle, you might point to a piece and say, "I think this is the piece we need for this space. Why don't you try it?" Then have the child pick up the piece and place it correctly. As the child becomes more aware of how the pieces fit into the puzzle, you can gradually withdraw your support.

- **Talk to your child, beginning at birth.** Your baby needs to hear your voice. Voices from a television or radio can't take the place of your voice, because they don't respond to your baby's coos and babbles. Your child needs to know that when he makes a certain sound, for example, "mamamamamama," that his mother will respond—he will smile and talk back to him. The more you talk to your baby, the more he will learn and the more he will have to talk about as he gets older.

Everyday activities provide opportunities to talk, sometimes in detail, about what's happening around him. As you give your child a bath, for example, you might say, "First let's stick the plug in the drain. Now let's turn on the water. Do you want your rubber duck? That's a good idea. Look, the duck is yellow.

- **Listen to your child.** Children have their own special thoughts and feelings, joys and sorrows, hopes and fears. As your child's language skills develop, encourage him to talk about his thoughts and feelings. Listening is the best way to learn what's on his mind and to discover what he knows and doesn't know and how he thinks and learns. It also shows your child that his feelings and thoughts are valuable.

- **Ask your child questions.** particularly questions that require him to give more than a "yes" or "no" response. If, as you walk with your toddler in a park, he stops to pick up leaves, you might point out how the leaves are the same and how they are different. With an older child, you might ask, "What else grows on trees?"

- **Answer your child's questions.** Asking questions is a good way for your child to learn to compare and to classify things—different kinds of dogs, different foods and so forth. Answer your child's questions thoughtfully and, whenever possible, encourage him to answer his own questions. If you don't know the answer to a question, say so. Together with your child, try to find the answer.

- **Read aloud to your child every day.** Children of all ages love to be read to—even babies as young as six weeks. Although your child doesn't understand the story or poem that you read, reading together gives him a chance to learn about language and enjoy the sound of your voice. You don't have to be an excellent reader for your child to enjoy reading aloud together. Just by allowing him to connect reading with the warm experiences of being with you, you can create in him a lifelong love of reading.

- **Be aware of your child's television viewing.** Good television programs can introduce children to new worlds and promote learning, but poor programs or too much TV watching can be harmful. It's up to you to decide how much TV and what kinds of shows your child should watch.

- **Be realistic about your child's abilities and interests.** Set high standards and encourage your child to try new things. Children who aren't challenged become bored. But children who are pushed along too quickly or who are asked to do things that don't interest them can become frustrated and unhappy.

- **Provide opportunities for your child to do and see new things.** The more varied the experiences that he has, the more he will learn about the world. No matter where you live, your community can provide new experiences. Go for walks in your neighborhood or go places on the bus. Visit museums, libraries, zoos and other places of interest.

If you live in small city, spend a day in the metropolitan city. If you live in the metropolitan city, spend a day in small city. Let your child hear and make music, dance and paint. Let him participate in activities that help to develop his imaginations and let him express his ideas and feelings. The activities in the next section of this book can provide your children with these opportunities.

CHAPTER 3

The Basics

The activities in this section are designed to help you prepare your child to learn and develop. Most of the activities are simple and easily can be made part of your daily routines. As you do the activities, remember that repetition is important, especially for very young children. Children enjoy—and learn—from doing the same activity over and over.

The activities are organized by the following age groups:

- Babies = Birth to 1 year old
- Toddlers = 1 to 3 years old
- Pre-schoolers = ages 3 to 5

All children are unique and learn at different pace. Keep in mind that all children don't always learn the same things at the same rate. And they don't suddenly stop doing one thing and start doing another just because they are a little older. So use the ages as guides as your child learns and grows and not as hard and fast rules. For example, an activity listed for the toddler age group may work well with a baby. On the other hand, the activity may not interest another child until he becomes a pre-schooler.

In addition, the activities change to meet the needs of children in the different age groups. Reading aloud activities are good examples. Reading aloud with your baby involves showing him a book and largely telling the story without placing too much emphasis on the actual written words. With older infants and toddlers, you stick closer to the written words and ask your child to identify or name pictures that go with the words. As your child develops language skills, you shift some of the story "reading" to him. When your child starts to recognize letters and perhaps words, you can call his attention to words that appear often or that he has learned to recognize from other reading.

Each section begins with a list of accomplishments and behaviors that are typical for the children in the age group. This is followed by a list of things that you can provide to help your child learn and grow. Again, because each child learns at his own rate, you should consider the lists only as guidelines.

As you use the activities, please remember the following points:

- **Some of these activities, although listed for a particular age group, are beneficial for children in all of the age groups.** Reading aloud, for example, is important to children from the time they are born. By modifying an activity, you enable your child to continue to enjoy it as he grows and develops.

- **Find activities that interest your child.** If you pick an activity that is too hard, your child may get discouraged. If it's too easy, he may get bored. Or if your child seems uninterested in an activity, try it again at some other time. Often children's interests change as they grow. Try to give your toddler or pre-schooler a choice of activities so that he learns to think for himself.

- **The activities are meant to be fun.** As you and your child do an activity, be enthusiastic and avoid lecturing to him about what he is learning and how important it is. If your child enjoys the activity, his excitement for learning will increase.

(a) Babies
(Birth to 1 Year Old)

What to Expect?
Babies grow and change dramatically during their first year. They begin to:

- Develop some control over their bodies. They learn to hold their heads up, roll over, sit up, crawl, stand up and, in some cases, walk.

- Become aware of themselves as separate from others. They learn to look at their hands and toes and play with them. They learn to cry when their parents leave and to recognize their own names.

- Play games. Babies first play with their own hands. Later they show an interest in toys, enjoy "putting in and taking out" games and eventually carry around or hug dolls or stuffed toys.

- Relate to others. Babies first respond to adults more than they do to other babies. Later they notice other babies, but they tend to treat these babies as objects instead of people. Then they pay attention when other babies make sounds.

- Communicate and develop language skills. Babies first cry and make throaty noises. Later they babble and say "mama" and "dada." Then they make lots of sounds and begin to name a few familiar people and objects. They begin to enjoy hearing rhyming and silly language.

What Babies Need?
Babies require:

- Loving parents or caregivers who respond to their cries and gurgles and who keep them safe and comfortable;

- Opportunities to move about and to practice new physical skills;

- Safe objects to look at, bat, grab, bang, pat, roll and examine;

- Safe play areas; and

- Many opportunities to hear language, to make sounds and to have someone respond to those sounds.

They learn to look at their hands and toes and play with them. They learn to cry when their parents leave and to recognize their own names.

1. Developing Trust
Feeling your touch, hearing your voice and enjoying the comfort of physical closeness all help your baby to develop trust.

What You Need?
- Music

What to Do?

- Gently move your newborn's arms and legs. Or tickle him lightly under the chin or on the tummy. When he starts to control his head, lie on the floor and put his head on your chest. Let him reach for your nose or grab your hair. Talk to him and name each thing that he touches.

- Place your baby on your belly. Some research has shown that such contact releases chemicals called *endorphins* that help your child feel comforted. In addition, such contact builds stomach and back muscle strength that is essential as your child learns to crawl.

- Sing and cuddle with your baby. Hold him snuggled in your arms or lying face up on your lap with his head on your knees. Make sure the head of a newborn is well-supported. Sing a favorite lullaby (a soft gentle song sung to make a child go to sleep).

- Include happy rituals in your baby's schedule. For example, at bedtime, sing the same songs every night, rock him or rub his tummy.

- Pick up your crying baby promptly. Try to find out what's wrong. Is he hungry? Wet? Bored? Too hot? Crying is your baby's way of communicating. By comforting him, you send the message that language has a purpose and that someone wants to understand him.

- To entertain your baby, sing an action song. For example:

  If you're happy and you know it, clap your hands!

  If you're happy and you know it, clap your hands!

  If you're happy and you know it and you want the world to know it,

If you're happy and you know it, clap your hands!

If you don't know lullabies or rhymes, make up your own!

- Dance with your baby. To soothe him when he's upset, put your baby's head on your shoulder and hum softly or listen to recorded music as you glide around the room. To amuse him when he's cheerful, try a bouncy tune.

> Babies need to become attached to at least one person who provides them with security and love. This first and most basic emotional attachment is the start for all human relationships.

2. Touch and See!

Whenever they are awake, babies are hard at work, trying to learn all about the world. To help them learn, they need many different things to play with and inspect. Objects you have around your home offer many possibilities.

What You Need?

- A wooden spoon with a face drawn on the bowl
- Different textured fabrics, such as velvet, cotton, corduroy, terry cloth, satin, burlap (a type of strong rough brown cloth, used especially for making sacks) and fake fur
- An empty toilet-paper or paper-towel roll
- Pots, pans and lids
- An old purse or basket with things to put in and take out
- Measuring cups and spoons
- Boxes and plastic containers
- Large spools (reel)
- Noisemakers (rattles, keys, a can filled with beans)

What to Do?

- Let your baby look at, touch and listen to a variety of objects. Objects that are brightly colored, have interesting textures and make noises are particularly good.
- Put one or two of the objects in a play area where your baby can reach them—more than two may confuse him. (Many of the objects will interest toddlers and older pre-schoolers. For example, babies love to inspect a paper towel roll. But a 4 year-old might use it as a megaphone for talking or singing, a telescope or a tunnel for a toy car).

Babies begin to understand how the world works when they see, touch, hold and shake things. Inspecting things also helps them to coordinate and strengthen their hand muscles.

3. Baby Talk

Babies love hearing the voices of the people in their lives.

What You Need?

- No materials are required

What to Do?

- Talk to your baby often. Answer his coos and gurgles. Repeat the "ga, ga's" he makes and smile back. Sometimes, you can supply the language for him. For example, when your baby stretches his arm towards his bottle and says, "ga ga-ga," say, "Oh, you're ready for some more milk? Here's your milk. Isn't it good!"

- Say or read to your child nursery rhymes or other verses that have strong rhythms and repeated patterns of sound. Vary your tone of voice, make funny faces and sing lullabies. Play games such as "peek-a-boo" and "pat-a-cake" with him.

- Play simple talking and touching games with your baby. Ask, "Where's your nose?" Then touch his nose and say playfully, "There's your nose!" Do this several times, then switch to an ear or knee or his tummy. Stop when he or you grow tired of the game.

- Change the game by touching the nose or ear and repeating the word for it several times. Do this with objects, too. When he hears you name something over and over again, your child begins to connect the sound with what it means.

- Point to and name familiar objects. By hearing an object named over and over, your baby learns to associate the spoken word with its meaning. For example, "Here's your blanket. Your very favorite blanket. What a nice, soft blanket!"

From the very beginning, babies try to imitate the sounds that they hear us make. They "read" the looks on our faces and our movements. Talking, singing, smiling and gesturing to your child help him to love—and learn to use language.

(b) Toddlers
(1 to 3 Years Old)

What to Expect?
Between their first and second birthdays, children:

- are energetic, busy and curious;
- are self-centered;
- like to imitate the sounds and actions of others (for example, by repeating words that parents and others say and by pretending to do housework or yard work with adults);
- want to be independent and to do things for themselves;
- have short attention spans if they are not involved in an activity that interests them;
- add variations to their physical skills (for example, by walking backwards);
- begin to see how they are like and unlike other children;
- play alone or alongside other toddlers;

- increase their spoken vocabularies from about 2 or 3 words to about 250 words and understand more of what people say to them;
- ask parents and others to read aloud to them, often requesting favorite books or stories; and
- pretend to read and write the way they see parents and others do.

Between their second and third birthdays, children:

- become more aware of others;
- become more aware of their own feelings and thoughts;
- are often stubborn and may have temper tantrums;
- able to walk, run, jump, hop, roll and climb;
- expand their spoken vocabularies from about 250 to 1,000 words during the year;
- put together 2-, 3- and 4-word spoken sentences;
- begin to choose favorite stories and books to hear read aloud;
- begin to count;
- begin to pay attention to print, such as the letters in their names;
- begin to distinguish between drawing and writing; and

- begin to scribble, making some marks that are like letters.

What Toddlers Need?

1 to 2-year-old children require:

- opportunities to make their own choices: "Do you want the red cup or the blue one?";
- clear and reasonable limits;
- opportunities to use large muscles in the arms and legs;
- opportunities to use small muscles to manipulate small objects, such as puzzles and stackable toys;
- activities that allow them to touch, taste, smell, hear and see new things;
- chances to learn about "cause and effect"—that things they do cause other things to happen (for example, stacking blocks too high will cause the blocks to fall);
- opportunities to develop and practice their language skills;
- opportunities to play with and learn about alphabet letters and numbers; and

- opportunities to learn about books and print.

2 to 3-year-old children require opportunities to:

- develop hand coordination (for example, by holding crayons and pencils, putting together puzzles or stringing large beads);

- do more things for themselves, such as dressing themselves;
- talk, sing and develop their language skills;
- play with other children and develop their social skills;
- try out different ways to move their bodies;
- learn more about printed language and books and how they work;
- do things to build vocabulary and knowledge and to learn more about the world, such as taking walks and visiting libraries, museums, restaurants, parks and zoos.

1. Shop Till You Drop

Shopping for groceries is just one of many daily routines that you can use to help your child learn. Shopping is especially good for teaching your child new words and for introducing him to new people and places.

What You Need?

- A grocery shopping list

What to Do?

- Pick a time when neither you nor your child is hungry or tired.

- At the grocery store, put your child in the grocery cart so that he faces you. Take your time as you walk up and down the aisles (a passage between rows of shelves in a supermarket).

- Let your child feel the items that you buy—a cold carton of milk, for example or the skin of an orange. Talk to your child about the items: "The skin of the orange is rough and bumpy. Here, you feel it."

- Be sure to name the objects that you see on shelves and talk about what you are seeing and doing: "First, we're going to buy some cereal. See, it's in a big red and blue box. Listen to the great noise it makes when I shake the box. Can you shake the box? Now we're going to pay for the groceries. We'll put them on the counter while I get out the money. The cashier will tell us how much we have to pay."

- Encourage your child to practice saying "hi" and "bye bye" to staff and other shoppers.

- Leave for home before your child gets tired or grumpy.

Children need to hear a lot of words in order to learn how to communicate. It's particularly helpful when you talk about the "here and now"—things that are going on in front of your child.

2. Puppet Magic

Puppets are fascinating to children. They know that puppets are not alive, yet they often listen to and talk with them as if they were real.

What You Need?

- An old, clean sock
- Buttons (larger than 1 inch in diameter to prevent swallowing)
- Needle and thread
- Red fabric
- Ribbon
- An old glove
- Felt-tipped pens
- Glue
- Yarn

What to Do?

- To make puppets:
    - *Sock puppet*: Use an old, clean sock. On the toe-end of the sock, sew on buttons for eyes and nose. Paste or sew on a piece of red fabric for the mouth. Put a bow made from ribbon at the neck.
    - *Finger puppets*: Cut off the fingers of an old glove. Draw faces on the ends of the fingers with felt-tipped pens. Glue on yarn for hair.
- Things to do with puppets:
    - Have the puppet talk to your child: "Hello. My name is Tanya. What's yours? Kareena. That's a

pretty name. What a great T-shirt you have on, Kareena! I like the rabbit on the front of your T-shirt." Or have the puppet sing a simple song. Use a special voice for the puppet.

- Encourage your child to talk to the puppet, answering its questions and asking questions of his own.
- Put finger puppets on your child's hand to give him practice moving his fingers one at a time.
- The next time you want your child to help you clean up, have the puppet make the request: "Hello, Mayank. Let's put these crayons back in the box and these toys back on the shelves. Can you get the ball for me?"

Puppets provide another opportunity for you to talk to your child and encourage him to talk to you as well. They also help your child to learn new words, use his imagination and develop hand and finger coordination.

3. Moving On
Toddlers love to explore spaces and to climb over, through and into things.

What You Need?
- Stuffed animal or toy
- Large board boxes
- Pillows
- A large sheet
- A soft ball
- A large plastic laundry basket
- Elastic
- Bells

What to Do?

- *Pillow Jump:* Give your child several pillows to jump into. (Toddlers usually figure out how to do this on their own).

- *Box Car:* Give your child a large cardboard box to push around the room. He may want to take his stuffed animal or toy for a ride in it. If the box isn't too high you'll most likely find your toddler in the box as well.

- *Basketball:* Sit about 3 feet away from your child and hold out a large plastic laundry basket. Let him try throwing a large, soft ball into the basket.

- *Table Tent:* Cover a table with a sheet that's big enough to reach the floor on all sides. This makes a great playhouse that's particularly good for a rainy day.

- *Jingle Bells:* Sew bells onto elastic that will fit comfortably around your child's ankles. Then watch (and listen) as he moves about or jumps up and down.

As you do an activity, talk, talk, talk with your child about what the two of you are doing!

4. Music Makers

Music is a way to communicate that all children understand. It's not necessary for them to follow the words to a song; it makes them happy just to hear the comfort in your voice or on the recording or to dance to a peppy tune.

What You Need?

- Music

- Noise makers (rattles, a can filled with beans or buttons, empty toilet paper rolls, pots, pans, plastic bowls)

What to Do?

- Have your toddler try banging a wooden spoon on pots, pans or plastic bowls; shaking a large rattle or shaking a securely closed plastic container filled with beans, buttons or other noisy items; and blowing through toilet-paper or paper-towel rolls.

- Sing or play recordings of nursery rhymes. Have your toddler participate actively. Even if he can't recite the words, he can imitate your hand movements, clap or hum along.

- As your child becomes more physically coordinated, encourage him to move to the music. He can twirl, spin, jump up and down, tiptoe or sway.

- Find recordings of all kinds of music for your child to listen to. Help him learn to clap out rhythms, to move to both slow and fast music and to listen carefully for special sounds in the music.

Here are a few tips to get your child to sing:

- Sing yourself. Sing fairly slowly so that your child can join in. Discourage shouting.

- Start with simple chanting. Pick a simple melody, such as "Mary Had a Little Lamb," and sing, "la, la, la." Add the words later.

- Make singing a natural part of your daily routine—let your child hear you sing as you work around the house or sing along with songs on the radio or TV or with your own CDs or recordings. Encourage him to join in.

Introduce music to your child early. Music and dance help children learn to listen, to coordinate hand and body movements and to express themselves creatively.

5. Play Dough

Young children love to play with dough. And no wonder! They can squish and pound it and form it into fascinating shapes. Helping to make play dough lets children learn about measuring and learn to use new words.

What You Need?

- 2 cups flour

- 1 cup salt

- 4 teaspoons cream of tartar

- 2 cups water

- 2 tablespoons cooking oil

- Food coloring

- Food extracts, such as almond, vanilla, lemon or peppermint

- Saucepan

- Objects to stick in the dough, such as Popsicle sticks and straws

- Objects to pound with, such as a toy mallet (wooden hammer)

- Objects to make impressions with, such as jar lids, cookie cutters and bottle caps

What to Do?

- To make play dough:

  - Add the food coloring to the water. Then mix all of the ingredients together in a pan.

  - Cook over medium heat, stirring until it forms a soft ball.

  - Let the mixture cool. Knead slightly. Add food extracts to different chunks of the dough to make different smells.

- Talk with your child about what you are doing as you make the dough. Let your toddler or pre-schooler help you with measuring and adding ingredients.

- Let your child handle some dough while it is still slightly warm and some when it has cooled off to teach him about temperatures.

- Give some of the dough to your toddler or pre-schooler so he can pound it, stick things in it, make impressions in it and make him own animals, houses and people from it.

Cooking with you—following the steps in a recipe—is the perfect way for your child to begin learning how to follow directions and how to count and measure. It can also teach him how things change.

6. Read to Me!

The single most important way for children to develop the knowledge they need to become successful readers later on is for you to read aloud to them often beginning when they are babies.

What You Need?

- Board books, predictable books and books that label and name concepts (such as colors, numbers, shapes)
- A children's dictionary (preferably a sturdy one)
- Paper, pencils, crayons, markers

What to Do?

- From the time your child is born, make reading aloud to your child a part of your daily routine. Pick a quiet time, such as just before you put him to bed. This will give him a chance to rest between play and sleep. If you can, read with him in your lap or snuggled next to you so that he feels close and safe. As he gets older, he may need to move around some as you read to him. If he gets tired or restless, stop reading. Make reading aloud a quiet and comfortable time that your child looks forward to.

- Try to read to your child every day. At first, read for no more than a few minutes at a time, several times a day. As your child grows older, you should be able to tell if he wants you to read for longer periods. Don't be discouraged if you have to skip a day or don't always keep to your schedule. Just get back to your daily routine as soon as you can. Most of all make sure that reading stays fun for both of you!

- Give your baby sturdy board books to look at, touch and hold. Allow him to turn the pages, look through the holes or lift the flaps. As your child grows older, have books on shelves or in baskets that are at his level. Encourage him to look through the books and talk about them. He may talk about the pictures and he may "pretend" to read a book that he has heard many times.

- For a late toddler or early pre-schooler, use reading aloud to help him learn about books and print. As you read aloud, stop now and then and point to letters and words; then point to the pictures they stand for. Your child will begin to understand that the letters form words and that words name pictures. He will also start to learn that each letter has its own sound—one of the most important things your child can know when learning to read.

- As you read, talk with your child. Encourage him to ask questions and to talk about the story. Ask him to predict what will come next. Point to things in books that he can relate to in his own life: "Look at the picture of the duck. Do you remember the duck we saw at the zoo?"

- Reread favorite books. Your child will probably ask you to read favorite books over and over. Even though you may become tired of the same books, he will enjoy and continue to learn from hearing them read again and again.

When reading books is a regular part of family life, you send your child a message that books are important, enjoyable and full of new things to learn.

- Read "predictable" books to your child. Predictable books are books with words or actions that appear over and over. These books help children to predict or tell what happens next. As you read, encourage your child to listen for and say repeating words and phrases, such as names for colors, numbers, letters, animals, objects and daily life activities. Your child will learn the repeated words or phrase and have fun joining in with you each time they show up in the story. Pretty soon, he will join in before you tell him.

- Be enthusiastic about reading. Read the story with expression. Make it more interesting by talking as the characters would talk, making sound effects and using facial expressions and gestures.

- Buy a children's dictionary—if possible, one that has pictures next to the words. Then start the "let's look it up" habit.

- Make writing materials such as crayons, pencils and paper available.

- Visit the library often. Begin making weekly trips to the library when your child is very young. See that your child gets his own library card as soon as possible. Many libraries issue cards to children as soon as they can print their names (you'll also have to sign for your child).

- Show your child that you read, too. When you take your child to the library, check out a book for yourself. Then set a good example by letting your child see you reading for yourself. Ask your child to get one of his books and sit with you as you read your book, magazine or newspaper. Don't worry if you feel uncomfortable with your own reading ability. It's the reading that counts. When your child sees that reading is important to you, he may decide that it is important to him.

- If you are uncomfortable with your reading ability, friends and relatives also can read to your child to do the same.

The books that you pick to read with your child are very important. If you aren't sure what books are right for your child, ask a librarian to help you choose titles.

(c) Pre-schoolers
(Children 3 to 5 Years Old)

What to Expect?
Between their third and fourth birthdays, children:

- Start to play with other children, interacting with them instead of the children next to them;

- Are more likely to take turns and share and begin to understand that other people have feelings and rights;

- Are increasingly self-reliant and probably can dress with little help;

- May develop fears ("Mommy, there's a monster under my bed.") and have imaginary companions;

- Have greater large-muscle control than toddlers and love to run, skip, jump with both feet, catch a ball, climb downstairs and dance to music;

- Have greater small-muscle control than toddlers, which is reflected in their drawings and scribbles;

- Match and sort things that are alike and unalike;

- Recognize numerals;

- Like silly humor, riddles and practical jokes;

- Understand and follow spoken directions;

- Use new words and longer sentences;
- Are aware of rhyming sounds in words;
- May attempt to read, calling attention to themselves and showing pride in their accomplishment;
- Recognize print around them on signs or in logos;
- Know that each alphabet letter has a name and identify at least 10 alphabet letters, especially those in their own names; and
- "Write," or scribble messages.

Between their fourth and fifth birthdays, children:

- Are active and have lots of energy and may be aggressive in their play;
- Enjoy more group activities, because they have longer attention spans;
- Like making faces and being silly;
- May form groups with friends and may change friendships quickly;
- Have better muscle control in running, jumping and hopping;
- Recognize and write the numerals 1-10;
- Recognize shapes such as circles, squares, rectangles and triangles;

- Love to make rhymes, say nonsense words and tell jokes;

- Know and use words that are important to school work, such as the names for colors, shapes and numbers; know and use words that are important to daily life, such as street names and addresses;

- Know how books are held and read and follow print from left to right and from top to bottom of a page when listening to stories read aloud;

- Recognize the shapes and names of all letters of the alphabet and know the sounds of some letters; and

- Write some letters, particularly those in his own name.

What Pre-schoolers Need
3 to 4-year-old children require opportunities to:

- play with other children so they can learn to listen, take turns and share;

- develop more physical coordination – for example, by hopping on both feet;

- develop their growing language abilities through books, games, songs, science, math and art activities;

- develop more self-reliance skills—for example, learning to dress and undress themselves;

- count and measure;

- participate actively with adults in reading-aloud activities;
- explore the alphabet and print; and
- attempt to write messages.

4 to 5-year-old children need opportunities to:

- experiment and discover, within limits;
- develop their growing interest in school subjects, such as science, music, art and math;
- enjoy activities that involve exploring and investigating;
- group items that are similar (for example, by size, color or shape);
- use their imaginations and curiosity;
- develop their language skills by speaking and listening; and
- see how reading and writing are both enjoyable and useful (for example, by listening to stories and poems, seeing adults use books to find information and dictating stories to adults).

1. Getting Along

Learning to get along with others is very important for children's social development.

What You Need?

- No materials required

What to Do?

- Give your child lots of personal attention and encouragement. Set aside time when you and your child can do enjoyable things together. Your positive feelings for your child will help him to feel good about himself.

- Set a good example. Show your child what it means to get along with others and to be respectful. Let him hear you say "please" and "thank you" when you talk to others. Treat people in ways that show you care what happens to them.

- Help your child find ways to solve conflicts with others. Help him to figure out what will happen if he shows his anger by hitting a playmate: "Junaid, I know that Amit took your truck without asking. But if you hit him and you have a big fight, then he will have to go home and the two of you won't be able to play any more today. What's another way that you can let Amit know you want your truck back?"

- Make opportunities for your child to share and to care. Let him take charge of providing food for birds. When new families move into the neighborhood, let him help make tea/cookies to welcome them.

- Be physically affectionate. Children need hugs, kisses, an arm over the shoulder and a pat on the back.

- Tell your child that you love him. Don't assume that your loving actions will speak for themselves (although they are very important).

Learning to work with and get along with others contributes to children's success in school.

2. Chores
Any household task can become a good learning game —and can be fun.

What You Need?

- Jobs around the home that need to get done, such as:
  - Doing the laundry
  - Washing and drying dishes
  - Carrying out the garbage
  - Setting the dinner table
  - Dusting

What to Do?

- Tell your child about the job you will do together. Explain why the family needs the job done. Describe how you will do it and how your child can help.

- Teach your child new words that are associated with each job: "Let's put the placemats on the table first, then the napkins."

- Doing laundry together provides many opportunities for your child to learn. Ask him to help you remember all the clothes that need to be washed. See how many things he can name: socks, T-shirts, pajamas, sweater, shirt. Have him help you gather all the dirty clothes, then help you make piles of light and dark colors.

- Show your child how to measure the detergent and have him pour the detergent into the washing machine. Let him put the items into the washing machine, naming each one. Keep out one sock. When the washer is filled with water, take out the mate to the sock. Let your child hold the wet sock and the one that you kept out. Ask him which one feels heavier and which one feels lighter. After the wash is done, have your child sort his own things into piles that are the same (for example, T-shirts, socks).

Home chores can help children learn new words, how to listen and follow directions, how to count and how to sort. Chores can also help children improve their physical coordination and learn responsibility.

3. Scribble, Draw, Paint and Paste
Young children are natural artists and art projects can spark young imaginations and help children to express themselves. Scribbling also prepares them to use writing to express their ideas.

What You Need?
- Crayons, water-soluble felt-tipped markers
- Different kinds of paper (including construction paper and butcher paper)
- Tape
- Finger paints
- Paste
- Safety scissors
- Fabric scraps or objects that can be glued to paper (string, cotton balls, sticks, yarn)

What to Do?

- Give your child different kinds of paper and different writing materials to scribble with. Coloring books are not needed. Crayons are good to begin with. Water-soluble felt-tipped marking pens are fun for your child to use because he doesn't have to use much pressure to get a bright color. Tape a large piece of butcher paper onto a tabletop and let your child scribble to his heart's content!

- Spread out newspapers or a large piece of plastic over a table or on the floor and tape a big piece of construction paper or butcher paper on top. Cover your child with a large smock or apron and let him finger paint.

- Have your child paste fabric scraps or other objects such as yarn, string or cotton balls to the paper (in any pattern). Let him feel the different textures and tell you about them.

- Here are a few tips about introducing your child to art:

  - Don't tell the child what to draw or paint.

  - Don't "fix up" your child's drawings. It will take lots of practice before you can recognize what he has drawn—but let him be creative! Invite your child to talk to you about what he is drawing and to identify by name each object in the picture.

  - Give your child lots of different materials to work with. Show him how to use new types of materials.

  - Find an art activity that's at the right level for your child and let him do as much of the project as possible.

  - Display your child's art prominently in your home. Point it out to visitors when your child is near to hear the praise

Art projects also help children to develop the eye and hand coordination they will later need as they begin to write.

4. Letters, Letters, Everywhere

Sharing the alphabet with children helps them begin to learn the letter names, recognize their shapes and link the letters with the sounds of spoken language.

What You Need?

- Alphabet book
- Alphabet blocks
- ABC magnets
- Paper, pencils, crayons, markers
- Glue
- Safety scissors

What to Do?

- With your child sitting with you, print the letters of his name on paper and say each letter as you write it. Make a name sign for him room or other special place. Have him decorate the sign.

- Teach your child "The Alphabet Song" and play games with him using the alphabet. Some alphabet books have songs and games that you can learn together.

- Look for educational videos, DVDs, CDs and TV shows that feature letter-learning activities for young children. Watch such programs with your child and join in with him on the rhymes and songs.

- Place alphabet magnets on your refrigerator or on another smooth, safe metal surface. Ask your child to name the letters he plays with and the words he may be trying to spell.

- Wherever you are with your child, point out individual letters in signs, billboards, posters, food containers, books and magazines.

- Encourage your child to spell and write his name. At first, he may use just a few letters for his name; for example, Sunny might use the letters SNY.

- Line up several alphabet blocks and have your child say the name of each letter. Have him use alphabet blocks to spell his name.

- Give your child a page from an old magazine. Circle a letter on the page and have him circle matching letters.

Children who know the names and the shapes of the letters of the alphabet when they enter school usually have an easier time learning to read.

5. Rhyme It!
Rhyming helps children start to pay attention to the sounds in words, which is an important first step in learning to read.

What You Need?
- Books with rhyming words, word games or songs

What to Do?
- Play rhyming games and sing rhyming songs with your child. Many songs and games include clapping and bouncing and tossing balls.

- Read nursery rhymes to your child. As you read, stop before a rhyming word and encourage him to fill in the blank. When he does, praise him.

- Listen for rhymes in songs that you know or hear on the radio, TV or at family or other gatherings. Sing the songs with your child.

- Around the home, point to objects and say their names, for example, sink. Then ask your child to say as many words as he can that rhyme with the name. Other good easily rhymed words are ball, bread, rug, clock and bread. Let him use some silly or nonsense words as well: ball—tall, call, small, dall, jall, nall.

- Say three words such as cat, dog and sat and ask your child which words sound the same—rhyme.

- If your child has an easy-to-rhyme name, ask him to say words that rhyme with it: Kate —plate, late, wait, date, gate.

- If a computer is available, encourage your child to download and run rhyming games.

Rhymes are an extension of children's language skills. By hearing and saying rhymes, along with repeated words and phrases, your child learns about spoken sounds and about words. Rhymes also spark a child's excitement about what comes next, which adds fun and adventure to reading.

6. Say the Sound

Listening for and saying sounds in words helps children learn that spoken words are made up of sounds, which gets them ready to match spoken sounds to written letters. This, in turn, gets them ready to read.

What You Need?

- Old magazine
- Book of nursery or nonsense rhymes

What to Do?

- Say four words that begin with the same sound, such as big, ball, basket and balloon.
- Ask your child to tell you the first sound in each word,/b/.
- Say four words, such as cap, hop, cake and camera. Ask your child which of the words starts with a different sound.
- Say four words, such as stop, top, mop and hop. Ask your child to tell you what the last sound is in each word,/p/.

- Give your child an old magazine. Sit with him and point out objects in the pictures. Ask him to say the sounds that the objects start with. Change the game by saying a sound and having him find an object in a picture that starts with that sound.

- Have fun by helping your child say tongue twisters such as "Peter Piper picked a peck of pickled peppers," and nonsense rhymes such as:
  - *Hey diddle diddle,*
  - *The cat and the fiddle,*
  - *The cow jumped over the moon,*
  - *The little dog laughed to see such sport,*
  - *And the dish ran away with the spoon.*
- As you read a story or poem, ask your child to listen for and say the words that begin with the same sound. Then have him think of and say another word that begins with the sound.
- Help your child to make up and say silly sentences with lots of words that start with the same sound, such as, "Tom took ten toy trucks to town."

Helping your child learn to pay attention to sounds in words can prevent reading problems later on.

7. Matching Sounds and Letters
Although children can be taught to match most letters with the sounds that they represent, be prepared to give them lots of help.

What You Need?
- Pieces of paper
- Paper bag

What to Do?
- Say some sounds for letters, such as/p/,/h/and/t/and have your child write the letter that matches the sound.
- As you read to your child, point out words that begin with the same letter as his name: Mohan/Megha and

morning, Lalit/Laxmi and land, Sunjay/Sonia and save. Have him find other words that begin with that sound.

- Write letters on pieces of paper and put them in a paper bag. Have your child take a piece of paper from the bag and say the name of the letter and the sound that it represents. Then have him say a word that begins with that sound.

- Sit with your child and play "I Spy." Look around the room and say, "I spy something that starts with/s/. What is it?" If you like, add clues such as "We use it to cook our food." (stove) "It's where we wash the dishes." (sink)

> Matching sounds with letters helps your child to learn that the letters he sees in written words represent the sounds he says in words. This is an important step in becoming a successful reader.

8. My Book

Many pre-schoolers like to talk and have a lot to say. Although most can't yet write words themselves, they enjoy dictating stories for others to write for them.

What You Need?

- Paper
- Paper punch
- Safety scissors
- Pencil, pen, crayons

- Yarn, staples

- Paste

What to Do?

- Make a booklet of five or six pages. Your child can help punch holes close to one edge and thread yarn through the holes to keep the pages together. You can staple the pages together.

- On the outside cover of the booklet, print your child's name. Explain to him that this is going to be a book about him.

- Let your child talk about what he will draw on each page. As he talks, print on the page what he says. Here are some examples:

  - Other people in my family
  - My favorite toys
  - My favorite books
  - My friends
  - My pet
  - My neighborhood
  - My home (or My bedroom)

- Encourage your child to read his books to family members and visitors.

Making this book will help your child develop both spoken and written language skills and give him more practice using the small muscles in his hands.

9. Hands-on Math

Hands-on activities that involve counting, measuring and using number words are a good way to introduce your pre-schooler to math.

What You Need?

- Blocks
- Dice

What to Do?

- Talk about numbers and use number concepts in daily routines with your child. For example:

  - "Let's divide the dough into two parts so we can bake some cookies now and put the rest of the dough in the freezer for cookies next week."

  - "We're going to hang this picture six inches above the bookshelf in your room. Let's use this ruler to measure."

  - "How many plates do we need on the table? Let's count: One for Mommy, one for Daddy and one for John. How many plates does that make? Three! Great!"

- Talk about numbers that matter most to your child— his age, his address, his phone number, his height and weight. Focusing on these personal numbers helps your child learn many important math concepts, including:

  - Time (hours, days, months, years; older, younger; yesterday, today, tomorrow). To a young child, you might say, "At 4 o'clock, we'll take a nap." When you plan with a pre-schooler, you could point out, "It's only three days until we go to Grandma's house. Let's put an X on the calendar so we'll know the day we're going."

- Lengths (inches, feet; longer, taller, shorter): "This ribbon is too short to go around the present for Aunt Simran. Let's cut a longer ribbon."

- Weight (milligrams, grams, kilograms; heavier, lighter; how to use scales): "You already weigh 12 kilograms. I can hardly lift such a big boy/girl."

- Where you live (addresses, telephone numbers): "These shiny numbers on our apartment/house door are 2-1-4. We live in apartment/house number 214." Or: "When you go to play at Tamanna's house, take this note along with you. It's our phone number: 25367104. Some day soon you will know our phone number so you can call me when you are at your friend's house."

• Provide opportunities for your child to learn math as he plays. For example:

- Playing with blocks can teach your child to classify objects by color and shape. Blocks can also help him to learn about depth, width, height and length.

- Playing games that have scoring, such as throwing balls into a basket, requires your child to count. Introduce him to games that use dice. Have him roll the dice and count the dots. Let him try to roll the dice and match numbers.

- Counting favorite toys.

Reading aloud counting books or books with number concepts can support your child's math learning.

□□□

CHAPTER 4

What About Kindergarten?

The activities in this book will help your child get ready for kindergarten. As the first day of school approaches, however, you may want to do a few more things to set your child on the path to school success.

1. **Find out if the school that your child will attend has a registration deadline.** Some schools have a limited number of slots for children. Start early to find out your school's policy and the procedures.

2. **Learn as much as you can about the school your child will attend before the school year begins.** Schools—even schools in the same zone/locality—can differ greatly. Don't rely only on information about kindergarten that you have received from other parents—their schools might have different

requirements and expectations. You will want to find out the following:

- The principal's name;
- The name of your child's teacher;
- What forms you need to fill out;
- What documents are required before your child enters school;
- A description of the kindergarten program;
- The yearly calendar and daily schedule for kindergarten children;
- Procedures for transportation to and from school;
- Available food services; and
- How you can become involved in your child's education and in the school.

Some schools will send you this information. In addition, some schools will hold orientation meetings in the spring for parents who expect to enroll their children in kindergarten the following fall. If your school doesn't plan such a meeting, call the principal's office to ask for information and to arrange a visit.

3.   **Find out in advance what the school expects from new kindergarten students.** If you know the school's expectations a year or two ahead of time, you will be in a better position to prepare your child. Sometimes parents and caregivers don't think the school's expectations are right for their children. For example, they may think that the school doesn't adequately provide for differences in children's learning and development or that its academic program is not strong enough. If you don't agree with your school's expectations for your child, you may want to meet with the principal or kindergarten teacher to talk about the expectations.

4. **Visit the school with your child.** Walk up and down the hallways to help him learn all the different rooms—his classroom, the library, the playground, the cafeteria. Let your child observe other children and their classrooms.

5. **Talk with your child about school.** During your visit, make positive comments about the school—your good attitude will rub off. ("Look at all the boys and girls painting in this classroom. Doesn't that look like fun!"). At home, show excitement about the big step in your child's life. Let him know that starting school is a very special event.

Talk with your child about the teachers he will have and how they will help him learn new things. Encourage your child to consider teachers to be wise friends to whom he should listen and show respect. Explain to your child how important it is to go to class each day. Explain how important and exciting the things that he will learn in school are—reading, writing, math, science, art and music.

6. **Consider volunteering to help out in the school.** Your child's teacher may appreciate having an extra adult to help do everything from passing out paper and pencils to supervising children on the playground. Volunteering is a good way to learn more about the school and to meet its staff and other parents.

When the long-awaited first day of kindergarten arrives, go to school with your child and be patient. Many young children are overwhelmed at first, because they haven't had much experience in dealing with new situations. They may not like school immediately. Your child may cry or cling to you when you say goodbye each morning, but with support from you and his teacher, this can change rapidly.

As your child leaves home for his first day of kindergarten, let him know how proud of him you are!

CHAPTER 5

Taking Charge of TV

By the time they begin kindergarten, children in the India have watched an average of 4,000 hours of TV. Most child development experts agree that this is too much. But banning TV from children's lives isn't the answer. Good TV programs can spark children's curiosity and open up new worlds to them. A better idea is for families and caregivers to monitor how much time their children spend watching TV and what programs they watch.

Here are some tips that will help you monitor and guide your child's TV viewing:

- Think about your child's age and choose the types of things that you want him to see, learn and imitate.

- Look for TV shows that:
  - teach your child something,
  - hold his interest,
  - encourage him to listen and question,
  - help him learn more words,
  - make him feel good about himself, and
  - introduce him to new ideas and things.

- Keep a record of how many hours of TV your child watches each week and what he watches. Some experts recommend that children limit their TV watching to no more than 2 hours a day. However, it's up to you to decide how much TV and what kinds of programs your child should watch.

- Learn about current TV programs, videos and DVDs and help your child to select good ones. Many other good children's programs are available on public television stations and on cable channels such as the Disney Channel and Nickelodeon.

- If you have a DVD player, you may wish to seek out video versions of classic children's stories and books.

- You can also read about programs in TV columns in newspapers and magazines. Cable subscribers and public broadcasting contributors can check monthly program guides for information.

- After selecting programs that are appropriate for your child, help him decide which ones he wants to watch. Turn on the TV when one of these programs starts and turn it off when the program ends.

- Watch TV with your child, so that you can answer questions and talk about what he sees. Pay special attention to how he responds, so that you can help him to understand what he 's seeing.

- Follow-up TV viewing with activities or games. Have your child tell you a new word that he learned from a TV program. Together, look up the word in a dictionary and talk about its meaning. Or have him make up his own story about one of his favorite characters from a TV program.

- Include the whole family in discussion and activities or games that relate to TV programs.

- Go to the library and find books that explore the themes of the TV shows that your child watches. Or help your child to use his drawings or pictures cut from magazines to make a book based on a TV show.

- Make certain that TV isn't used as a babysitter. Instead, balance good television with other enjoyable activities for your child.

CHAPTER 6

Choosing

Choosing the right kind of childcare for your baby, toddler or pre-schooler is important for your child's safety and well being. It is also important because these early experiences affect how prepared your child is for school. Here are some tips to guide you in choosing childcare:

- Think about the kind of care that is best for your child. Some possibilities to consider are (a) a relative; (b) a day-care provider, usually someone who takes care of a small group of children in his own home; (c) a childcare center, which generally offers a curriculum and staff with educational backgrounds in early childhood development; and (d) a caregiver who comes to your home.

- Decide which kind of childcare fits your budget.

- Start looking for childcare early, particularly if you have a special program for your child in mind. Some programs have long waiting lists.

- Gather information. Whether you are looking for a day-care provider or for a caregiver to come into your home, interview the person at length and check references carefully. Before you meet with the person, develop a list of questions. If you are considering day-care centers, visit each one —more than once. Don't rely only on good reports about the center from other people. Centers that work well for other parents may not work well for you. As with any kind of childcare, check the center's references carefully.

No matter what kind of childcare you are considering, look for care providers who:

- **Are kind and responsive.** Good care providers enjoy being with children, are energetic, patient and mature enough to handle crises and conflicts.

- **Have experience working with young children and like them.** Find out how long the providers have worked with pre-schoolers, why they are in the child-care field and whether they provide activities that are appropriate for your child's age. Observe the providers with other children. Do the children seem happy? How do the providers respond to them?

- **Recognize the individual needs of children.** Look for care providers who are considerate of different children's interests and needs and who can provide your child with enough attention.

- **Have a child-rearing philosophy that is similar to your own.** Find out what kind of discipline the providers use and how they handle problems.

Be certain that the childcare facility is clean and safe. Check to see that it is full of equipment and materials that will allow your child to explore and learn, including plenty of books and separate areas of different kinds of activities.

Centers that work well for other parents may not work well for you. As with any kind of childcare, check the center's references carefully.

CHAPTER 7

Ready-For-School Checklist

The following checklist, although not exhaustive, can help to guide you as you prepare your child for school. It's best to look at the items on the list as goals towards which to aim. They should be accomplished, as much as possible, through everyday routines or by enjoyable activities that you've planned with your child. If your child lags behind in some areas, don't worry. Remember that children grow and develop at different rates.

Good Health and Physical Well-Being
My child:

- Eats a balanced diet
- Gets plenty of rest
- Receives regular medical and dental care
- Has had all the necessary immunizations
- Runs, jumps, plays outdoors and does other activities that help develop his large muscles and provide exercise
- Works puzzles, scribbles, colors, paints and does other activities that help develop his small muscles

Social and Emotional Preparation
My child:

- Is learning to explore and try new things interacts with others

- Is learning to work well alone and to do many tasks for himself

- Has many opportunities to be with other children and is learning to cooperate with them

- Is curious and is motivated to learn

- Is learning to finish tasks

- Is learning to use self-control

- Can follow simple instructions

- Helps with family chores

Language and General Knowledge
My child:

- Has many opportunities to talk and listen

- Is read to every day

- Has access to books and other reading materials
- Is learning about print and books
- Has his television viewing monitored by an adult
- Is encouraged to ask questions
- Is encouraged to solve problems
- Has opportunities to notice similarities and differences
- Is encouraged to sort and classify things
- Is learning to write his name and address
- Is learning to count and plays counting games
- Is learning to identify and name shapes and colors
- Has opportunities to draw, listen to and make music and to dance
- Has opportunities to get first-hand experiences to do things in the world—to see and touch objects, hear new sounds, smell and taste foods and watch things move

Early Learning and Childhood Basics

It's fascinating to watch young children learn about their world and develop new skills. And, it's natural to find variation in the pace of development of different skills. The information and resources in this section will help parents and educators understand and support preschool-aged children's development.

Early Literacy

It is critical to help young children be ready for school by working with them to develop early literacy and learning skills. Strong reading skills form the basis for learning in all subjects, so it is important to identify those who struggle with reading as early as possible.

Early Math

During the preschool years children build a foundation of math skills and learn a wide-range of math concepts. Just as a child learns about words by learning the alphabet and letter sounds, learning how to do math begins with learning what numbers are and then how to count.

Preschoolers (3-5 years of age)

Developmental Milestones

Skills such as naming colors, showing affection, and hopping on one foot are called developmental milestones.

Developmental milestones are things most children can do by a certain age. Children reach milestones in how they play, learn, speak, behave, and move (like crawling, walking, or jumping).

As children grow into early childhood, their world will begin to open up. They will become more independent and begin to focus more on adults and children outside of the family. They will want to explore and ask about the things around them even more. Their interactions with family and those around them will help to shape their personality and their own ways of thinking and moving. During this stage, children should be able to ride a tricycle, use safety scissors, notice a difference between girls and boys, help to dress and undress themselves, play with other children, recall part of a story, and sing a song.

POSITIVE PARENTING TIPS

Following are some things you, as a parent, can do to help your preschooler during this time:

- Continue to read to your child. Nurture her love for books by taking her to the library or bookstore.
- Let your child help with simple chores.
- Encourage your child to play with other children. This helps him to learn the value of sharing and friendship.
- Be clear and consistent when disciplining your child.
- Explain and show the behavior that you expect from her. Whenever you tell her no, follow up with what he should be doing instead.
- Help your child develop good language skills by speaking to him in complete sentences and using "grown up" words.
- Help him to use the correct words and phrases.
- Help your child through the steps to solve problems when she is upset.

- Give your child a limited number of simple choices (for example, deciding what to wear, when to play, and what to eat for snack).

Child Safety First

As your child becomes more independent and spends more time in the outside world, it is important that you and your child are aware of ways to stay safe. Here are a few tips to protect your child:

- Tell your child why it is important to stay out of traffic. Tell him not to play in the street or run after stray balls.

- Be cautious when letting your child ride her tricycle. Keep her on the sidewalk and away from the street and always have her wear a helmet.

- Check outdoor playground equipment. Make sure there are no loose parts or sharp edges.

- Watch your child at all times, especially when he is playing outside.

- Be safe in the water. Teach your child to swim, but watch her at all times when she is in or around anybody of water (this includes kiddie pools).

- Teach your child how to be safe around strangers.

- Keep your child in a forward-facing car seat with a harness until he reaches the top height or weight limit allowed by the car seat's manufacturer. Once your child outgrows the forward-facing car seat with a harness, it will be time for him to travel in a booster seat, but still in the back seat of the vehicle.

HEALTHY BODIES

- Eat meals with your child whenever possible. Let your child see you enjoying fruits, vegetables, and whole grains at meals and snacks.

- Your child should eat and drink only a limited amount of food and beverages that contain added sugars, solid fats, or salt.

- Limit screen time for your child to no more than 1 to 2 hours per day of quality programming, at home, school, or child care.

- Provide your child with age-appropriate play equipment, like balls and plastic bats, but let your preschooler choose what to play. This makes moving and being active fun for your preschooler.

BEST SELLING TITLES OF GPH

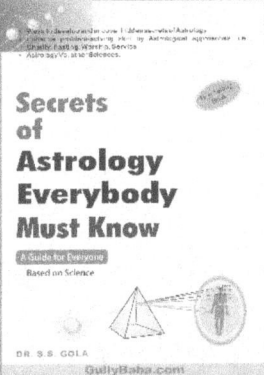

www.ingramcontent.com/pod-product-compliance
Lightning Source LLC
Chambersburg PA
CBHW072018170626

46813CB00005B/2178